Easter Bunny Fables

3 stories by Matt Gabriel Bench
Illustrations by Pete Berg

Printed in the U.S.A.

Library of Congress Control Number 2015907353
ISBN #987-1511766883

Published by:
Humble Bee Books
PMB A-3 • 621 SR 9 NE • Lake Stevens WA 98258

Easter Bunny Fables:
Three heartwarming fables that include valuable lessons, such as, it's OK to be different; pride and humility; and unconditional love.

Upcoming Humble Bee Books include:
Purple Gold: An orphan's boys trials turns to gold.
The Party: Everyone's invited to the party, but who will come?

Come visit us at:
www.humblebeebooks.com

Ester Bunny

Story by

Matt Gabriel Bench

Illustrations by

Pete Berg

Printed in the U.S.A.

Library of Congress Control Number: 2008910439
ISBN #1-4392-1820-X

Published by:

Humble Bee Books

PMB A-3   •   621 SR 9 NE   •   Lake Stevens WA 98258

Ester Bunny:
A heartwarming and inspiring folk tale depicting the origin of the Easter Bunny.

Upcoming Humble Bee Books include:

Evan Bunny: Ester's grandson battles with pride
Purple Gold: An orphan boy's trials turns to gold.
Ella Bunny: Will hard times steal Ella's joy or will Ella rise to the occasion?

To view the previews you may visit
www.humblebeebooks.com

Ester Bunny is...

Dedicated to my mother, Shirley Bench,

who encouraged me to dream and modeled true blue values.

A special thank you to my loving and dedicated wife Sandy;

to my children, Ethan, Tyler, and Holly

for whom the story was created;

to my encouraging friend Sheila Dunn;

and to my awesome Selix family relatives in South Dakota.

Also a special thanks to my brother Jeff Bench

for his "Golden" touch in my life

and for providing the final edits for Ester Bunny.

The proud rooster signaled the
start of another new day on the Selix
farm with a mighty cock-a-doodle-do!!!
Thaddeus Selix, the father of the nine Selix children,
sat hunched on his stool milking the cows. The plow mule and
the family horse rested in the barn. The pigs played tag in the mud,
while the chickens in the hen house kept clucking away, laying their
eggs. The Selix children bustled through the house, and around
the farm, rows of corn stalks stretched out to greet the morning sun
peeking over the horizon.

This day would
be no ordinary day,
for on this day,
near the creek that
bordered the Selix
farm, a very special
little bunny was
born. Her parents,
Delores and Walter,
named her Ester.

Ester, unlike other bunnies, grew up with a great imagination.
As a youngster, she was drawn to the beauty she saw in butterflies.
When she was old enough for chores, her chore was to gather
food. Ester always looked for food near the different
berry bushes.

To Ester, the berry bushes looked very beautiful. The salmon berries shone orange like the brilliance of the setting sun. The raspberries tumbled down the vines knit together like soft red pillows. The blueberries?...well, the blueberries were of course...blue, a deep, dark, radiant blue. Ester would sit for hours looking at the different colors and shapes of the berries. When Ester talked to her bunny friends about the beautiful berries, they just laughed at her. The somewhat older bunnies scolded her for staring at the berries instead of doing her chores.

The next afternoon when Ester went out to gather food, she very quietly picked some blueberries, wrapped them in big leaves, and brought them home to her hutch. Each day she gathered food, she very quietly and carefully picked another type of berry and brought it home. She did this until she had collected a batch of each kind of berry. But on her last trip home, she was greeted by a very grumpy-looking older bunny named Frump. Frump was not happy about his blue tail. Frump had sat on a stack of Ester's blueberries and stained his tail blue. Ester thought Frump's tail looked very pretty, but that just made Frump even angrier. Frump said some mean things to Ester, which made her sad.

But wait...
Frump's blue tail gave
her a great idea! Ester
suddenly imagined
how she could make
all sorts of things look
pretty by squishing
berries on them, and
hopped up and down
in excitement.

Ester continued
to gather berries. In
her free time, she
would find flat gray rocks from the creek and drag
them back to her hutch. After the rocks dried, she
squished the berries on them to make lovely patterns
of blue, red and orange.

As Ester grew older, she became a master at painting with berries. She used her front paw as a paintbrush. She discovered that she could use blades of grass to make the color green, and with wild mustard plants, she could make the color yellow. She also discovered she could use cornhusks, chicken feathers, and other ordinary things she found around the Selix farm to make patterns. She created her favorite painting on a flat rock shaped like a half-moon. She painted the rock blue and put a yellow star on it. Then she dipped a cornhusk in red raspberries and rolled it across the bottom of the rock in a way that made a cobblestone pattern.

As beautiful and original as Ester's paintings were, bunnies simply do not usually think art is important. In the village where Ester lived, the bunnies could not understand why she spent all of her free time painting. Some bunnies just left her alone, others made fun of her behind her back, and some teased her. A few, including Frump, were downright mean to Ester because she was different. Ester became very sad and discouraged.

To keep from being teased or hurt, she decided to quit painting. She packed up all of her painting supplies and began dragging them to the creek. She picked up pack after pack and tossed them into the creek. Each time she threw a pack, she cried a little harder. When she tossed the last pack into the creek, she sat on its bank and sobbed.

The sun soon set, casting rays of pink, orange, and purple across the sky. Still, Ester was sad. Then along came Golden who put his big paw on Ester's back. Golden was one of the oldest and most respected bunnies in the village. He rarely spoke, but when he did, words of wisdom always came out of his mouth. Golden talked to Ester about why the other bunnies acted the way they did. He told Ester, "The other bunnies are good deep down inside, but they can not understand why you are so different." Golden encouraged Ester to continue painting and agreed to help her find a place to paint where the other bunnies would not bother her.

The next day, Ester and Golden set out to find the right spot for Ester's new painting place. They spent most of the day looking. They looked in hollow logs, they looked in fields, they looked all over, but they could not find the right spot. Their legs were aching, and they were ready to quit for the day when they noticed two of the Selix children playing outside the barn. Shirley and Ted were tossing berries at each other, trying to catch them in their mouths.

Right between Ted and Shirley, Ester spotted a small opening in the barn where the bottom of a board was broken off. Ester had a good feeling, and talked Golden into looking through the opening to see where it went. After Shirley and Ted ran off, Ester and Golden

quickly hopped to the opening in the barn and wiggled inside. Once inside, they saw they were in an empty horse stall. It was perfect! Ester became very excited and began hopping up and down. This would make a fine painting place with many places to store berries, grass, mustard plants, pattern makers and rocks.

Ester could not hide her excitement. She spent all of her free time during the next month gathering a new supply of painting materials. She was only able to gather a few flat gray rocks, since they were heavy and hard to carry all the way from the creek to the barn. Then, as luck would have it (some might say it was the hand of God) the strangest thing happened. A chicken wandered into the barn, ran over to Ester's painting place, laid a white egg, and then ran out of the barn. Ester stared at the egg, and what do you think she thought?

That's right! She thought, "This egg is perfect for painting."
Ester quickly scooped up some berries and began to paint the egg.
WOW! The colors looked very bright on the white egg, and with her
pattern makers, she could make designs that wrapped all the way
around the egg. Ester was "soooooo" excited. She hopped all over
the barn, bumping into things. She even knocked over the
pitchfork, which bounced so hard on an upside-
down milking bucket that
it sounded like a drum.

After
Ester calmed
down, she
decided to
risk going
over to the
chicken coop to
find some
more eggs. She

quietly hopped by the
farmhouse, quickly hopped past the pigs
playing in the mud, and cautiously hopped by the
watchful rooster. Into the chicken coop she went.
She carried a small pack with her.

Risking being seen by the chickens, she carefully opened her pack of berries and started painting away. She made red eggs, orange eggs, blue eggs, eggs with wavy patterns, eggs with dots, and eggs with many colored stripes. Before she knew it, she painted over 30 eggs, and the chickens did not seem to care at all. They just kept clucking away, having a grand time.

The sun was going down and Ester could not wait to tell Golden of her new discovery. When she got back to the main bunny hutch by the creek, she ran smack into Frump. Frump would not let Ester past him. He questioned Ester until she told him about painting all the eggs. Frump tried to scare Ester by telling her, "When the Selix family finds the colored eggs they will be very mad." When Ester heard this, she became afraid. She hopped back to the chicken coop as fast as her tired legs would carry her. What was Ester to do? Her heart was pounding with fear. She could not let the Selix family find the colored eggs. She would have to hide all the colored eggs before the Selix children came to gather them in the morning.

By this time, it was dark outside. Ester had a hard time seeing anything, but one by one, she carried the eggs out of the chicken coop and hid them. She hid them under plants. She hid them under the front porch. She hid them next to the pigpen. She hid them behind bales of hay. She even hid some in the cornfields.

When Ester finished, it was almost morning and she was plumb tuckered out. She started back, but she was so tired that before she reached the barn, she could not take another step and fell fast asleep. She fell into a deep sleep. When the rooster crowed an hour later, she

did not hear him. She also did not hear Shirley Selix come out of the farmhouse earlier than usual to gather eggs to allow the Selix family to leave on time for Easter service.

Yes, it was Easter morning. Shirley came back out of the chicken coop looking quite puzzled. She wondered, "What had happened to all the eggs?" Then Shirley caught sight

of a red egg under the spruce tree. Shirley called to her brothers and sisters to come out and see the red egg. Lucille Selix saw the next egg, a blue one with yellow spots. The search was on. The nine Selix children had a joyous time finding all the colored eggs. While looking, they also found Ester and her painting place. Ester was covered in colors from head to tail. The Selix children wondered if this bunny had painted all the eggs. The colors matched. "The patterns looked as if they came from the pattern makers found in Ester's painting place.

When Ester saw how very happy the children were with her painted eggs, she knew right away that she was doing what she was meant to do. The Selix family shared the story of Ester, the bunny who painted chicken eggs and hid them, so they could have fun hunting colored eggs on Easter morning. The news spread fast, and before long, everyone in town wanted to have a colored egg hunt on Easter morning. As years went by, Ester taught many boy and girl bunnies how to paint and hide what we now know as Easter eggs. Because Ester did not give up on her unique dreams and talents, the world was blessed with *Ester, the first Easter Bunny*.

PARENT/TEACHER GUIDE:

Often, what some people view as a weakness or a problem is really a strength or an ability. If properly encouraged, children, like Ester, can develop their unique qualities into assets.

QUESTIONS TO ASK YOUR CHILD/CHILDREN OR STUDENTS:

How was Ester different from other bunnies?

How did the other bunnies first act toward Ester?

How did Ester feel when other bunnies teased her and were mean to her?

What would have happened if Ester stopped painting when the other bunnies teased her?

Do you think it helped Ester to have the wise bunny Golden encourage her to continue painting?

Talk to your child/children or students about something you like about them that is unique. If nothing immediately comes to mind, some qualities you may suggest include: artistic, kind to others, generous, smart, musical, coordinated/athletic, joyful, attentive, creative, good at figuring out how things work, good at making things, good with animals, imaginative, bring out the best in others, and adventurous.

May your adventure in helping your child or students discover and explore their unique talents be joyous and rewarding.

Evan Bunny

Story by
Matt Gabriel Bench

Illustrations by
Pete Berg

Printed in the U.S.A.

Library of Congress Control Number: 2009903727
ISBN #1-4392-3745-X

Published by:

Humble Bee Books

PMB A-3   •   621 SR 9 NE   •   Lake Stevens WA 98258

Evan Bunny:
Sequel to *Ester Bunny*. A winning story about pride, humility and second chances

Upcoming Humble Bee Books include:
Ester Bunny: Released 2008, a heartwarming and inspiring folk tale depicting the origin of the Easter Bunny
Ella Bunny: Will hard times steal Ella's joy or will Ella rise to the occasion?
Purple Gold: An orphan boy's trials turns to gold

To view the previews you may visit
www.humblebeebooks.com

 *Evan Bunny* is...

Dedicated to my sisters, Becky, Sandy, and Mary.
I have always felt their love and encouragement.

A special thank you to Pete Berg
for another wonderfully illustrated book.

A special thank you to my brother, Jeff Bench,
for editing Evan Bunny.

A special thank you to Jen, Adam, Kim and Holly
for providing great input to the story.

Most of all, thank you to my wife Sandy,
who truly is my better half.

**The Brookville Easter Parade
bubbled with activities —**

clowns riding unicycles, bands playing lively
music, balloons swaying, and children laughing.

The gleeful crowd cheered as the Mayor awarded Ester a shiny certificate of courage and proclaimed her the official Easter Bunny. The Mayor then pulled back a tarp to unveil a beautiful bronze statue of Ester carrying a basket filled with colorful Easter eggs. The cheers grew as Ester was showered with a rainbow of streamers.

The Mayor hushed the cheering crowd and spoke, saying, "Ester showed great courage in using her unique God-given talents to follow her dreams of being a great artist. Even when others greatly discouraged her, she still succeeded."

The Mayor ended his speech by saying, "In honor of Ester Bunny, each year, just before Easter, a contest will be held to select a bunny who best represents Ester's character and talents to be that year's official Easter Bunny." The cheers from the crowd erupted once again, lasting several minutes as the parade came to a close.

Ester was often asked what it was like to be the first Easter Bunny.

Ester was quick to say how grateful she was for a wise bunny named Golden whose help and encouragement was so important when other bunnies were not nice to her. She also would explain, though it wasn't always easy for her, everything, both easy and hard, had to happen in just the right order and at just the right time for her to become the Easter Bunny.

She was quoted as saying "I could not have planned a better ending if I had tried. I was truly blessed."

Easter egg hunts became so popular that bunnies became instant superstars. The bunny selected official Easter Bunny for the year was treated like royalty.

Remaining humble is hard when so much honor and attention gets heaped on a bunny. The Easter Bunny was pampered and groomed. He would also hear praise like, "Easter Bunny, oh how beautiful you are", "We love you", and "Can we have your pawto-graph?"

Imagine trying to remain humble if you were Ester's grandson. Well, Evan was just that bunny.

You see, Evan was Ester's grandson and he was a glorious looking bunny. His fetaures were very handsome. His fur shone like an auburn sun and felt as soft as a gentle breeze.

From the day he was born, Evan often heard that he was sure to be crowned the official Easter bunny one day.

Evan was known for being good hearted. However, because of all of the special attention, he started to think he was more special than other bunnies. He started expecting everyone to give him special treatment and started to take his friends for granted. Can you imagine a bunny barking? Well, Evan's demanding voice sounded like he was barking out orders to his friends.

"Mic, fetch me some berries! Lollamore, brush my fur! White Cloud, get me something to eat!" Evan stopped listening to others, including his friends. He thought, 'why waste my time listening to them when what I have to say is much more important?'

Of course, what Evan had to say was not more important and he was wrong to treat his friends badly. As a result he lost many friends.

The signs of the fall season coming to a close and the beginning signs of winter were everywhere. The farmers had harvested all of their crops and taken them to market. The morning air turned crisp, causing the bunnies' noses to twitch. The evening sun took on a muffled glow as it appeared to bundle up and bow goodnight.

As winter swept in, excitement arose when those bunnies who had dreams of being crowned the next official Easter Bunny came from near and far to attend the Fine Bunny Academy. Here, bunnies were taught what they needed to know when competing for the crown and most importantly, the expectations of the official Easter Bunny.

Fine Bunny Academy

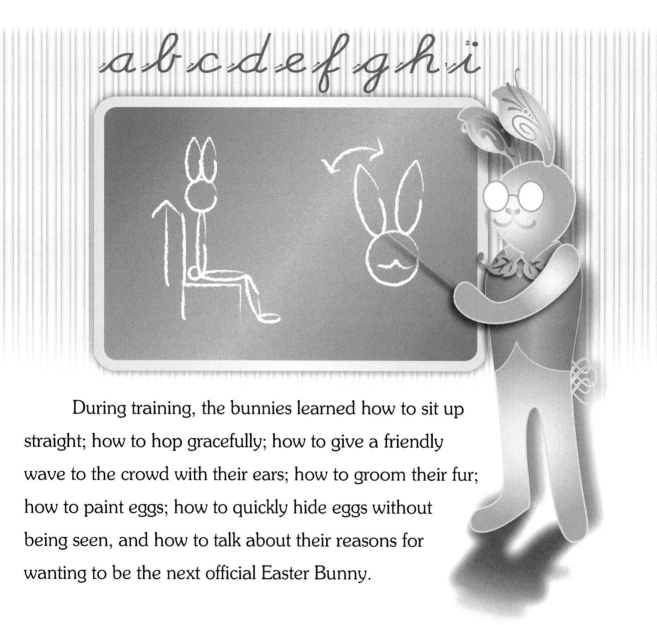

During training, the bunnies learned how to sit up straight; how to hop gracefully; how to give a friendly wave to the crowd with their ears; how to groom their fur; how to paint eggs; how to quickly hide eggs without being seen, and how to talk about their reasons for wanting to be the next official Easter Bunny.

The expectations of the official Easter Bunny, better known as "C" training, were also taught. "C" training stood for character, commitment, and courage. Bunnies would learn the importance of being humble, being giving and not greedy, and having the courage to always do the right thing.

A crowd gathered as a parade of Easter Bunny hopefuls hopped by to enroll in the Fine Bunny Academy. Eyes throughout the crowd widened and jaws fell open in amazement at how beautiful the bunnies were. The hopefuls included Lilly Lop from Longview; Heather Hare from over the hill; Sandy Bunny from Frontier Village; Fin Rabbit from across the water, and many others. As grand as these bunnies were, they were no match for Evan. But where was Evan?

Evan had decided he was too good for the Fine Bunny Academy. He fugured it was just a waste of time, because he was sure to win anyway. Pride had overcome him.

The Fine Bunny Academy training finished just in time for the Easter Bunny contest. The contest began with all the bunnies hopping by, waving and smiling. Heather and Lilly's furs were so shiny that their coats appeared to glow. Even without the special training, Evan's coat looked wonderful. All the bunnies showed their special talents. Laddy from Larue hid his eggs so fast and skillfully that the judges did not even notice he had started before he was done. Fin's egg coloring ability was really special. Only Evan with the training he received from Ester was able to match Fin in egg coloring. The events came to a close.

The scores were added and five finalists were selected. The finalists were Heather, Lilly, Fin, Laddy, and Evan. In turn, each Bunny was asked,

"Why do you want to be the official Easter Bunny?" Heather said it was a life long dream of hers. Lilly talked about the joy of making people happy. Fin described his wish to be a role model. Laddy simply stated it would be a lot of fun. It was Evan's contest to win. With a heartfelt answer the crown would be his. The question was asked, "Evan, why do you want to be the official Easter Bunny?" Evan's pride welled up as he said "Because I am the best and I deserve it."

The final votes were in. The Mayor himself read the results.

With a loud clear voice the Mayor announced, "Third place goes to...Lilly." Lilly graciously accepted her award.

The Mayor then announced,

"Second place goes to Heather." Heather clapped her ears and hopped up to receive her award. Evan started forward to receive the first place crown when the Mayor once more called out in his booming voice, "The new...Easter Bunny of Brookville is... Fin Bunny." Fin did a double back flip as he bounded up and accepted the crown.

Evan, stunned and embarrassed, hung his head and slunk off the stage. No bunny saw him after that. His few loyal friends looked and called for him, but could not find him.

Now in her elder years, Ester had become quite wise. She had a feeling she might know where to find Evan.

Ester remembered how much Evan liked it when she taught him how to paint so she hopped back to the barn where her old painting place could be found.

She called out for Evan, but no answer came. Ester gently hopped into the old horse stall and softly called out once again. This time, Evan popped his head up from underneath the hay.

Ester and Evan talked for hours. Ester gave great advice and Evan saw how foolish he was for letting himself become so prideful. Ester and Evan spoke many times after that where Evan learned many valuable character lessons and finally regained his good heart. Ester encouraged Evan to compete again the next year to be the official Easter Bunny. Evan said "NO WAY!"

Ester kept encouraging Evan, telling him it would take true humility and courage to try again. Evan finally agreed to try once more.

Evan began helping his neighbors and treating his friends with respect. He also enjoyed just having fun playing with the other bunnies. Evan's actions showed that he had learned from his mistakes.

The next winter season arrived and this time Evan took the right hops. He enrolled in the Fine Bunny Academy and signed up for the Brookville Easter Bunny contest.

When the contest was held, Evan used the training and advice he received to give his best effort. A handsome and smiling Evan hopped past the judges giving a perfect bunny ear wave. His egg painting and hiding skills were the best. In fact, the results were not even close. The judges scored Evan first in every event. The finalists were selected and the moment of truth came when Evan was asked, "Why do you want to be the Easter Bunny?" Evan honestly replied "I have been blessed with a second chance and I am humbled to be considered for the honor. If I win, I only hope to be a good representative of all the bunnies around the world."

Evan sat quietly as the Mayor stepped up to the microphone. After reading off the third and second place finishers the Mayor was ready to announce the winner. With his booming voice he shouted, "The new official Ester Bunny of Brookville is Evan..." and before he could say "Bunny," the crowd jumped up cheering loudly. The Mayor, grinning from ear to ear, placed the crown onto a very humble and honored Evan Bunny.

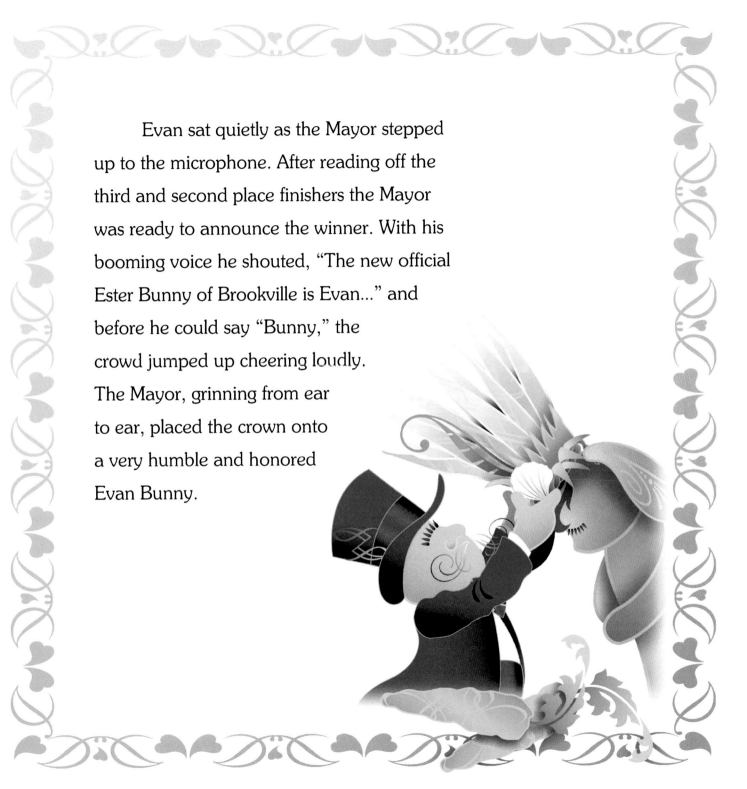

Pride had caused Evan to lose many friends and the first contest. After being humbled, he learned from his mistakes, regained his good heart, and showed courage to try again. In the end, Evan became a true friend and champion to all.

Way to go Evan!

PARENT/TEACHER GUIDE:

DEFINITIONS:

Prideful (in this story) – Feeling superior to others. Having a higher opinion of oneself than earned. Having an "I deserve it" attitude.

Humble – modest, respectful, courteous, without pride.

QUESTIONS TO ASK YOUR CHILD/CHILDREN OR STUDENTS:

What were the reasons Evan did not attend Easter Bunny prep school before the first contest?

Was it a wise choice by Evan to not attend Easter Bunny prep school before the first contest? Why or why not?

If you are good at something, would it help you to get more practice and training to get even better? Why?

After Evan lost the first contest, what do you think would have happened if Ester had not encouraged him to try again?

What do you think would have happened if Evan remained prideful and was not able to humble himself?

What does this statement mean: Pride comes before a fall?

You may choose to have a discussion about pride, humility, failure, and success. Ask your child/children or students if they remember times when others were prideful. How did it make them feel? Ask them if they remember times when others were humble. How did it make them feel? *(refer to the above definitions to help the children understand the question.)*

You may choose to have a conversation about failure and success. Some youth feel like they have failed or do not meet expectations. Share: even if a person does not succeed at something, they are not a failure unless they totally give up. Thomas Edison was not successful 99 times before he succeeded in inventing a light bulb that worked. What would have happened if he had never tried or had given up beofre his 100th attempt?

Ella Bunny

Story by
Matt Gabriel Bench

Illustrations by
Pete Berg

Printed in the U.S.A.

Library of Congress Control Number: 2009903620
ISBN #1-4392-3675-5

Published by:

Humble Bee Books
PMB A-3 • 621 SR 9 NE • Lake Stevens WA 98258

Ella Bunny: Will hard times steal Ella's joy or will Ella rise to the occasion?

Upcoming Humble Bee Books include:
Ester Bunny: Released December 2008, a heartwarming and inspiring folk tale depicting the origin of the Easter Bunny
Evan Bunny: Released July 2009, sequel to *Ester Bunny*. A winning story about pride, humility and second chances
Purple Gold: An orphan boy's trials turns to gold

To view the previews you may visit
www.humblebeebooks.com

Ella Bunny is...

Dedicated to my earthly father Frank Bench
and to my Heavenly Father.

A special thank you to Jeff Bench for editing *Ella Bunny*
and to Jen Jolliff for providing great input.

A big hug to my wife Sandy who daily demonstrates
her unconditional love for me.

And a special thank you to Pete Berg who brought the
Ester Bunny, *Evan Bunny*, and *Ella Bunny* stories to life
with his anointed and skillful illustrations.

Children's laughter echoed throughout the town

and over the hills as the annual Brookville Easter celebration ended with the popular Easter egg hunt and painting contest.

Ethan won the award for the most eggs found for the second year in a row. What were the odds of that? Tyler won the best sport award for helping other children find eggs; even though it meant he found fewer eggs for himself. Holly won the "WOW" egg award for the most original and beautiful egg. Somehow, she made her egg sparkle like an emerald.

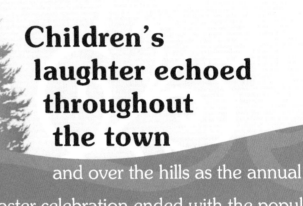

The Easter egg
hunt and painting
contest had become
so very popular,
mainly because of
the amazing work of
the Easter bunnies. The best Easter
bunnies received their training at

The Fine Bunny Academy

where the finest teachers were located.

Laddy from Larue taught there and passed on his secrets for hiding eggs quickly and without being seen. Laddy was so good at not being

seen that they nicknamed him the Invisible Bunny. The famous Ester Bunny had taught students how to be good bunny role models. Evan Bunny's lessons on character were taught, but he was most known for making up fun games with fair rules.

His favorite rules were those he made for hopscotch. Evan's hopscotch rules included the flip-flop toss the rock rule and the double hop criss-cross rule. The host of the hopscotch game called out the rules he or she wanted. More often than not, when watching the bunnies play hopscotch, one would hear the host bunny just call out "Evan's Rules" because they were the fairest and most fun.

A feeling of happiness was almost always present in Brookville, and especially at the Fine Bunny Academy. When did this happen and where did it start? It was not clear at first, but *every* bunny noticed the change. If a bunny really thought about it, he or she could put two hops, a skip and a bunny jump together and *see* that it started right about the time Ella Bunny came to teach at the Fine Bunny Academy.

Her upbeat hop was enough to make others glad to see her. Her expressive eyes lit up the sky and made others feel special. When she spoke, everyone could feel her love. Nothing ever got Ella down, and before long every bunny in the community had picked up his or her hop and was happy: every bunny that is except Furrow Bunny.

Furrow was known for scaring other bunnies into doing what he wanted them to do. He would tell bunnies things that would make them afraid. Then he would tell them he would protect them if they would do things for him. The bunnies did not like Furrow's attitude, but they did not know how to change it. Ella made other bunnies feel so good they would forget about being afraid, and that made Furrow angry.

Furrow started thinking about what he could do to make other bunnies afraid again in order to regain his control. He thought and thought. As he thought, he wondered, what would my great-great-grandpa Frump have done?

What is the biggest event in Brookville? OH NO! He did not possibly think about wrecking the grand Easter egg hunt, or did he? Yes, indeed Furrow had come up with a plan to make the other bunnies afraid and wreck the grand Easter egg hunt. Then he would make himself look like a hero for "saving the day."

The next year, as Easter came closer, Furrow began his terrible plan. Furrow lied by saying he heard the Mayor say the chickens were sick, and it would not be safe to touch them or their eggs. Furrow also gave out fake flyers noting the Easter egg hunts would have to be canceled. He even put the Mayor's name on the bottom of the flyers to make them look official.

As the terrible news spread, every bunny's happiness turned into sadness: every bunny that is except Ella. Ella kept her hop high, her eyes bright, and her words uplifting. The other bunnies wondered how Ella could still be happy when the news was so sad.

One bunny named
Morgan asked Ella how she
could still be happy when
every other bunny was so sad?
Ella answered, "Oh, you have
happiness mixed up with joy.
While I AM a happy bunny,
what you see in me comes
from pure joy." Morgan asked,
"What is the difference?" Ella
replied, "Joy does not come
from the outside or from
what happens around us like
happiness does. Joy comes
from the inside and from
knowing you are loved with a
love that will never fail."

Morgan asked, "How did you get that kind of joy? Ella answered, "As far back as I can remember, my Father would always tell me he loved me and nothing would ever change his love for me. He said, no matter what I did, no matter how good or bad I was, no matter how well I performed, he loved me with a love that would last forever and always. I know this is true."

Ella continued, "One time I did something I knew was wrong. I was really hungry and I stole some carrots from my neighbor. My Father found out and he was not happy with me. He made me tell my neighbor I was sorry and made me do extra work, but he also gave me a great big bunny hug and told me he loved me.

"Because I know I have a Father who loves me and true joy comes from knowing you are loved, nothing on this earth can take my joy away."   Morgan whispered, "But aren't you afraid of touching the eggs from the sick chickens?" Ella replied, "Pure love defeats fear, every time. Besides, those chickens look healthy to me."

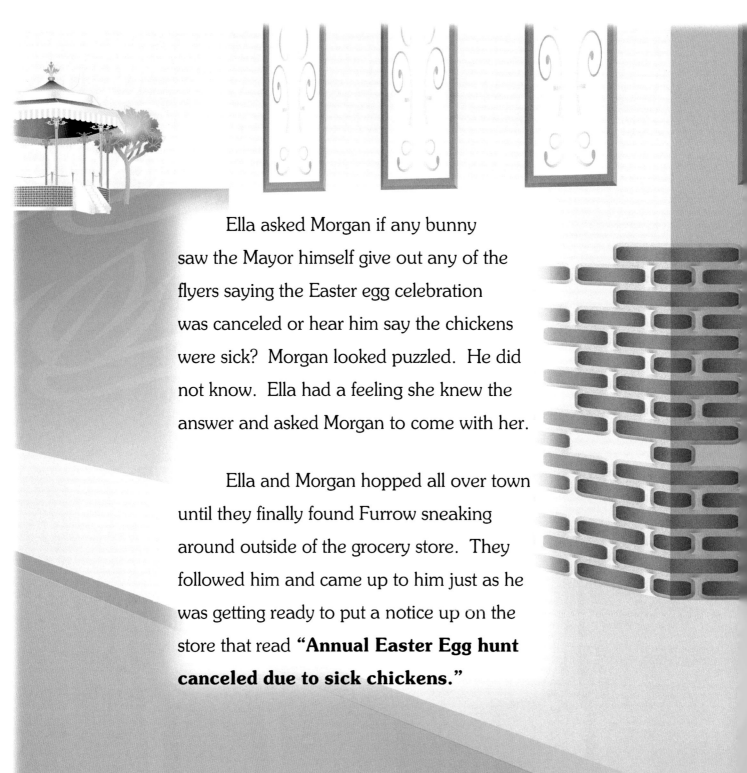

Ella asked Morgan if any bunny saw the Mayor himself give out any of the flyers saying the Easter egg celebration was canceled or hear him say the chickens were sick? Morgan looked puzzled. He did not know. Ella had a feeling she knew the answer and asked Morgan to come with her.

Ella and Morgan hopped all over town until they finally found Furrow sneaking around outside of the grocery store. They followed him and came up to him just as he was getting ready to put a notice up on the store that read **"Annual Easter Egg hunt canceled due to sick chickens."**

Morgan and Ella questioned Furrow. Furrow began telling his lies, but as he looked into Ella's loving eyes he found he could not help but tell the truth. Furrow finally admitted the notices he was posting were fake and they were part of his terrible plan to make the bunnies sad and afraid.

He also told them about the rest of his plan to tell everyone he had the cure for the sick chickens and if they would make him the head bunny he would heal the sick chickens and save the Easter egg hunt.

Then, Ella looked directly into Furrow's eyes and said, "Furrow, even though you have done a very bad thing, I still love you," and gave him a great big bunny hug. Furrow felt the hug all the way to the center of his heart. Furrow sobbed. No bunny had ever shown him pure love before. Furrow told Morgan and Ella how sorry he was and asked them to forgive him. Ella, in her soft loving voice said, "Yes, I forgive you Furrow." Morgan fussed a little, kicked the ground, twitched his ears, and then slowly said in a scrunched up voice "Yes, I forgive you too."

The Annual Brookville Easter Egg Hunt

Don't miss the Annual Easter Egg Hunt!

Furrow, Morgan, and Ella went around town and took down all the fake flyers and notices. More importantly, they spread the news that the grand annual Easter celebration would once again have the Easter egg hunt, with the painting contest as the main event.

Furrow was forever a changed bunny. He volunteered more hours than any other bunny to help make the Easter celebration the best ever. As the story is told, Furrow left Brookville the next year to start Easter egg parades in many towns. Some say, because of his great love for others, that he learned and experienced from Ella, he even became the Honorary Mayor of Pleasanton.

Ella Bunny moved on the next year. Morgan and the other bunnies begged her not to go, but she simply said, "My work here is done, but you will always have a special place in my heart." The lessons Ella taught lived on and on, and to this day, Brookville is one of the most joyous towns on the planet.

PARENT/TEACHER GUIDE:

Note to Parent/Teacher: It will be important to note that some of the children may not have an earthly father at home. Depending upon the venue, you can assure the children they will always have a Heavenly Father who loves them.

QUESTIONS TO ASK YOUR CHILD/CHILDREN OR STUDENTS:

Why did Furrow try to make the other bunnies afraid?

When Ella gave Furrow a great big bunny hug filled with love, what did it do for Furrow?

Why was Ella able to keep her happiness and joy when the other bunnies became sad?

Ella said her joy came from knowing her Father loved her. Not all children have an earthly father living in the home. What can take the place of an earthly father's love? (Mother, grandparent, caring adult, Heavenly Father)

Do you know you are just as special as Ella? You are a true treasure of God and He loves you no matter what.

If someone tries to make you afraid or is mean to you, what do you think you should do? (Answer: show them kindness in return. Maybe they just need a big bunny hug because they are not feeling loved)

What do you think the MORAL of the story is?
Answer: Love is stronger than fear and truth is more powerful than lies. Having the love of the Father is more powerful than anything. And, nothing can take true joy away because it comes from a love that will never fail.

Made in the USA
Middletown, DE
02 February 2021

32866461R00049